Astral Legacy

TANISH NAIR

Copyright © 2024 Tanish Nair

Dedication

To my mother,

Your unwavering support and guidance have been the foundation of my journey. You have always encouraged me to experiment, learn on my own, and gain invaluable experience. Your relentless push for me to excel in every aspect, coupled with the wisdom and ideals you instill, has shaped my life profoundly. For all this and more, I am eternally grateful.

Preface

As an avid reader, I've always found solace and excitement in the pages of my favourite books. Fictional worlds like those in Percy Jackson, Harry Potter, and the Inheritance Cycle have been my constant companions, offering me adventures beyond my wildest dreams. These stories have not only entertained me but also sparked my imagination, igniting a creative fire within me.

Over the years, I've read countless books, each one leaving its mark and inspiring me in unique ways. Gradually, I started to envision my own stories, filled with characters and worlds that were yearning to be brought to life. This book is the culmination of those ideas—a blend of inspiration from the beloved tales of Percy Jackson and the Inheritance Cycle, interwoven with my own imagination.

Writing this story has been a journey, one that allowed me to explore new realms and breathe life into the characters and adventures that have been dwelling in my mind. I hope that this book will transport you to a world of wonder and excitement, just as my favorite books have done for me.

Thank you for joining me on this adventure. Happy reading!

Tanish Nair

At GLAM AUTHOR, we help children publish their first book.

To publish you child's book, contact us

+91 8698790004

Prologue

In the realm of **Sköllgard**, four ancient kingdoms have flourished for centuries, each endowed with unique elemental powers that shape the land they inhabit. From the towering peaks of the south-eastern mountains to the sun-scorched deserts of the south-west, the kingdoms of **Inferno Dominion, Thunderlash, Glacierborns, and Terrashifters** command the forces of nature and wield their strengths in distinct territories.

In the distant past of Sköllgard, during the Epoch of Harmony an ancient relic of the nature gods was unearthed by curious humans seeking forbidden knowledge. This relic, a sacred artifact once belonging to a revered nature deity, held immense power, and was intended to safeguard the balance of the natural world. However, when the humans attempted to use this relic in a misguided ritual, they unwittingly disrupted the delicate harmony between realms.

As the ritual unfolded, rifts tore open between the mortal realm and the ethereal realm of the nature gods. Through these rifts, the nature deities crossed over into the mortal world, their energies mingling with certain individuals and endowing them with elemental powers.

Four distinct clans emerged from this transformative event, each aligned with a fundamental force of nature.

However, not all lineages received these divine blessings. Those untouched by the elemental powers were shunned and marginalized, consigned to lives of servitude and hardship within the kingdoms of birth. They became known as the **"Nulls"**, ostracized from society and forbidden from mingling with the empowered clans.

In today's Age of Ascendence at the north-western front of Sköllgard lies the Inferno Dominion, a realm of blazing plains and fertile valleys bathed in perpetual sunlight. Here, the soil is rich and bountiful, yielding abundant harvests and sustaining thriving communities. The Inferno Dominion is known for its mastery over fire and heat, harnessing these elements to fuel their forges and cultivate the land. They could be recognized by the distinctive rune on their neck.

To the southeast, where the land rises into rugged mountains veiled in perpetual ice and snow, the Glacierborns reign supreme. These resilient people control the frozen wilderness, channelling the power of frost and ice to shape the glaciers and rivers that cascade down from their lofty peaks. The ancient river that winds through their domain bears the name "Borealistra," its icy waters a lifeline for both the Glacierborns and the creatures that roam their snowy lands. They have a rune on their forearm.

Thunderlash Tribe

The Glacierborns

The Terrashifters

Inferno Dominion

In the northeast, sprawling across vast plateaus and

rolling hills, lies the domain of Thunderlash. Its dramatic thunderstorms and electrified skies characterize the kingdom. The Thunderlash warriors command the power of lightning, using it to protect their highland homes and strike fear into their enemies. The plateaus of the tribe are known for their strategic importance and natural fortifications. The people of the Thunderlash have a rune on their shoulder.

Lastly, in the southwestern reaches of Sköllgard, the Terrashifters rule over the expansive desert wastes. Enduring the scorching heat and shifting sands, they possess a deep connection with the earth and its secrets. The Terrashifters manipulate sandstorms and seismic forces, reshaping the desert landscape to their advantage. They possess a rune on their calf.

Amidst the sprawling landscapes of Sköllgard, there existed secluded and forgotten corners of the land that remained aloof and distant from the bustling societies of the elemental controllers. These enigmatic regions were inhabited by reclusive inhabitants who held themselves apart, viewing the practitioners of elemental powers with a mixture of curiosity and disdain. They regarded the elemental controllers as primitive beings.

These secluded regions deep beneath the rugged terrain hidden from the prying eyes of the surface dwellers of Sköllgard harboured arcane knowledge, guarded by the guardians of the forgotten lands. There exists an enigmatic community known as the Craftweavers. These skilled artisans and weapon makers dwell in subterranean chambers, their forges glowing with the heat of molten metal as they craft weapons of unparalleled quality and power. The Craftweavers are a secretive lot, rarely seen or heard by outsiders, for they have chosen a life of seclusion and dedication to their craft.

The denizens of the Craftweaver community serve a unique purpose in the realm of Sköllgard—they forge weapons not for mere mortals, but exclusively for the strong and influential figures among the human populace. Kings, warlords, and champions seek out the Craftweavers for their exceptional craftsmanship and the potent magic infused into each blade and armor piece they create.

Far above the subterranean world of the Craftweavers lies the ancient and venerable Enlightened Community of the Southern Forest—the Loreweavers. These wise and contemplative individuals dedicate their entire lives to the pursuit of knowledge and enlightenment. They meditate in serene groves, attuning their minds to the whispers of nature and the secrets of the cosmos.

Painful echoes of Realisation

The balance of power among the elemental clans is defined by ancient lineage and the legacy of war that has shaped their history. At the pinnacle of strength stand the Inferno Dominion and the Thunderlash tribe, renowned for their mastery over fire and lightning, respectively. Over time, their rivalry evolved into a tenuous alliance driven by a shared ambition for dominance.

Seeking to solidify their united strength and maintain supreme control, the Inferno Dominion and the Thunderlash tribe formed an alliance, namely the Thundering Flame Alliance, forging a formidable bond that reverberated across the realm.

The weaker Terrashifters and Glacierborns found themselves no match for the formidable alliance. As the Inferno Dominion and Thunderlash solidified their bond, the Terrashifters and Glacierborns faced increasing oppression and hardship.

The Terrashifters struggled under the weight of the Inferno Dominion's fiery dominance. Similarly, the Glacierborns, masters of frost and cold, were outnumbered and outmatched by the Thunderlash tribe's lightning-fuelled prowess.

To strengthen their alliance and ensure the future unity of their clans, it was decided that the strongest members of each family would come together in marital union. Ignatius Vulcan, a towering figure known for his strength, pride, and ruthless valor, represented the Inferno Dominion. His mastery over fire was unparalleled, wielding a sword infused with the fiery essence of Sköllgard itself—a weapon that blazed with power and devastation.

Opposite him stood Fulminari Volta of the Thunderlash tribe, a majestic and beautiful figure whose calm demeanor belied her merciless competence. She was unforgiving in battle, wielding a trident infused with thunderous power and the ability to command the weather itself. Fulminari's presence commanded respect and fear, her eyes holding the secrets of storms and lightning.

As the alliance solidified through their marital union, whispers of prophecy and destiny swirled in the air.

With great excitement and anticipation, a child was born to Ignatius the Magnificent of the Inferno Dominion, and Fulminari Volta of the Thunderlash tribe.

They named him Cassian Vulcan, after the greatest ancestor of the Inferno.

However, Cassian's birth took them by surprise. It brought disappointment and regret instead of celebration. Unlike the expectations of his lineage, Cassian bore no elemental mark on his shoulder from the Thunderlash, nor any rune around his neck from the Inferno Dominion. Instead, he possessed an unidentifiable, empty eye-like rune—a mysterious symbol that defied understanding.

Cassian's lack of elemental prowess was seen as a curse and a bad omen by his clans. Considered an outcast and a symbol of misfortune, he was forced to leave the fertile plains of the Inferno Dominion and seek exile in the mountains.

Cassian was ignored, looked down upon, and shunned by others like him who bore no elemental marks. In the mountains, he found himself isolated and without guidance. At a very young age, he was left to fend for himself, lacking skills and proper teaching. To make matters worse, Cassian was weak, thin, and plagued by constant illness, further isolating him from any semblance of community or support.

As Cassian embarked on his solitary journey through the unforgiving valleys beneath the Thunderlash plateau, he encountered a landscape that echoed the rugged majesty. The ravines stretched wide and deep, their rocky walls rising sharply on either side, casting long shadows that concealed hidden dangers.

He hunted for sustenance among the sparse vegetation, relying on his meager skills to catch small game and gather whatever edible plants he could find. Water was a precious commodity, and whenever he stumbled upon the shores of Niflheimr Lake, he savored the cool, refreshing respite it offered.

Journeying aimlessly for days, unsure of his destination, Cassian eventually reached the foothills of the ginormous Cryoros Peaks where the Glacierborns resided, and he climbed to the top of a small hill to gain a better view of the path ahead. As he spent the night there, gazing up at the vast expanse of stars, something within him stirred. The stars seemed to call out to him, pulling him into their celestial dance. Cassian felt an inexplicable fascination and connection with the stars— they became his solace, his refuge from a world that had rejected him.

In the quiet solitude of that hilltop, Cassian found solace and a sense of purpose. He began to love the stars, finding comfort in their silent presence and the sense of belonging they offered him. Unlike the judgmental eyes of his fellow beings, the stars welcomed him without prejudice or scorn. This newfound passion ignited a spark within Cassian.

Cassian immersed himself fully in the study of the stars, dedicating his days and nights to mapping their movements, tracing constellations, and discovering hidden patterns in the celestial dance above. His passion for astronomy consumed him, becoming the sole purpose of his life amidst the harsh solitude of the mountains.

On the night Cassian turned 12, unaware of the significance of his age, he was gazing up at the sky when suddenly, an odd flicker caught his attention amidst the stars. A dim, faint twinkle appeared and then a star vanished without a trace. At that moment, the empty eye-like rune on Cassian's back burned intensely, causing him great pain. The searing sensation was so overwhelming that Cassian lost consciousness.

As Cassian drifted into unconsciousness, he heard an oddly familiar voice whispering in the depths of his mind. It was a faint voice, almost like an echo from a distant memory, repeating a name—Eldris. The voice was elusive, and amidst the haze of pain and darkness, Cassian could barely discern the repeated murmur of "Eldris, Eldris, Eldris."

When Cassian finally regained awareness, he found himself lying beneath the starlit sky, the pain subsiding but the memory of the mysterious voice lingering in his thoughts. The events of that night left Cassian with more questions than answers, his mind consumed by the cryptic experience and the burning sensation of the rune on his back.

Driven by a desire to unravel the mystery behind his burning rune, Cassian resolved to journey deeper into the mountains, seeking a civilization that might accept him and offer him insights to interpret the reason for the recent events.

The rugged terrain of the Cryoros Mountains loomed before him, their icy peaks shrouded in mist. Cassian trekked along ancient trails, his steps guided by determination and the faint hope of discovery.

As Cassian traversed through the dense, cold valleys of the mountains, a monstrous creature known as a Wolfsbane ambushed him. This fearsome beast, massive like a bear yet swift and agile as a wolf, bore down on Cassian with razor-sharp fangs and menacing teeth. Cassian, weakened by sickness and unable to defend himself, desperately tried to escape the creature's deadly grasp.

Just as the Wolfsbane lunged for Cassian, its jaws poised to strike, a sudden and unexpected intervention saved him. A spear-like icicle launched with precision and power and pierced through the beast's eye with incredible force. The Wolfsbane let out a pained roar as the icy spear impaled its skull, exiting through the other side.

Cassian, shocked and relieved, turned to see who had come to his rescue. Standing before him was a figure clad in furs and ice, wielding a staff adorned with frozen runes—a member of the Glacierborns, skilled in the art of ice magic and guardianship of their mountainous domain.

The Glacierborn warrior approached Cassian, her expression stern yet curious. "Are you injured?" she asked, her voice echoing with the chill of the snowy landscape.

Cassian, still shaken but grateful, managed to reply, "No, I... I think I'm okay. Thank you for saving me."

The Glacierborn warrior nodded and remarked, "These usually do not attack, wonder what got into it" " her piercing gaze scanning Cassian's face. "What brings you to our lands, traveller? You do not appear to be one of us."

Cassian hesitated, then mustered the courage to speak of his recent experiences—the mysterious disappearance of stars, his transformative encounter beneath the celestial sky, the whispering message about Eldris. He did not talk about the rune on his back for fear of being cast away again. The Glacierborn listened intently, her demeanor softening with understanding.

"You seek answers," the Glacierborn said thoughtfully. "Come with me. Our elders may have the knowledge you seek."

With a mix of relief and curiosity, Cassian followed the Glacierborn deeper into the snowy wilderness.

The Serpent's Summoning

In the heart of the Inferno Dominion stood a grand citadel, The Inferno Citadel. It was a manifestation of its fiery legacy. Perched majestically upon the fertile plains of the Inferno Dominion, a colossal structure of the purest Ruby and flame-tempered steel, the palace commands the horizon with its imposing presence.

Massive gates, forged from the finest fire-infused metals, guard the entrance to the citadel. Each gate is emblazoned with ancient runes that shimmer with an inner fire, symbolizing the eternal strength of the Inferno Dominion. At the threshold, colossal statues of fire giants stand sentinel, their eyes ablaze with flickering flames, a formidable warning to any who dare approach with ill intent.

Beyond the gates lay a diamond-laden court that rose taller than a giant. Here, in this majestic two-storeyed hall, King Vulcan the Magnificent held court as he sat 10 steps above all his courtiers. His presence commanded awe and respect, his fiery aura matching the intensity of the flames that danced around him.

On this auspicious day, 11 years after Cassian's exile, Vulcan awaited the arrival of a distinguished guest—the ruler of the Thunderlash tribe, King Ragnor the Tempest. Ragnor, known for his mastery over thunder and storms, approached with regal grace. His presence was accompanied by the crackle of distant thunder, a testament to his elemental prowess.

As Ragnor entered the fiery ruby-laden hall, the air seemed to electrify with anticipation. The two kings, Vulcan and Ragnor, met in the heart of the Inferno Dominion.

In the imposing court of the Inferno Dominion, Ragnor of Thunderlash and Vulcan of Inferno Dominion exchanged nods, acknowledging the weight of their meeting.

"Solgra, Ragnor," Vulcan greeted, his voice resonant in the vast hall.

"Aelkhar, Vulcan," Ragnor replied, his gaze steady.

Silence lingered briefly before Vulcan spoke again. "How fares Thunderlash, Ragnor? Your people are resilient."

Ragnor's expression softened slightly. "We endure Vulcan. Days get brighter with each passing hour."

Vulcan's eyes narrowed with concern. "And your daughter, Fulminari? She leads with strength and conviction, does she not?"

Ragnor nodded slowly. "Indeed, Fulminari is a beacon of hope for our tribe. But the challenges ahead weigh heavily on her."

Ragnor's brow furrowed in concern. "Storms have passed over Thunderlash, but the air remains charged. And what of your son, Ignatius? Is he prepared for the task ahead?"

Vulcan's gaze hardened with pride. "Ignatius has grown strong, Ragnor. He wields the flame with unmatched vigor, ready to fulfill his destiny."

Vulcan's continued "Raging fires are kept at bay, yet the embers smolder."

Ragnor nodded, acknowledging the shared emotions. "Our people yearn for stability, Vulcan. Sköllgard teeters on the brink."

Vulcan's eyes bore into Ragnor's. "We cannot afford another misstep, Ragnor. The consequences would be dire."

Ragnor's jaw tightened with resolve. "Indeed, Vulcan. We must take decisive action. The time for half-measures has passed."

"I propose a daring plan, Ragnor. One that requires unity and unwavering resolve." Said Vulcan, eyes gleaming with determination.

"We must take an unexpected path, Ragnor," Vulcan began, his voice low yet resolute. "Something beyond the ordinary measures."

Ragnor's curiosity piqued, and he leaned forward slightly. "What do you propose, Vulcan?"

Vulcan's gaze shifted, a glint of purpose in his eyes. "We require a power greater than any single clan possesses."

"And what could that be?" Ragnor said.

Ragnor's brow furrowed in thought. "You speak of the ancient Thraex of Niflheimr Lake!? How do you intend to subdue and extract that monster let alone use it? Our strength alone may not suffice. "

Witnesses speak of a dreadful aura emanating from this beast, a palpable sense of impending doom that freezes the hearts of even the bravest souls. Its haunting cries echo across the land, a cacophony of eerie wails that seem to call forth forgotten terrors from the depths of history.

Vulcan's expression darkened slightly. "We must take bold action. I will dispatch a cavalry with Ignatius to the Terrashifter domain. Meanwhile, you must send Fulminari with an army contingent to the glacierborn palace."

Ragnor's eyes widened with realization. "To… kidnap… their… leaders... This is a daring plan, Vulcan."

Vulcan's voice lowered to a near whisper. "We must harness the combined might of Thunderlash, Inferno Dominion, the Glacierborns, and the Terrashifters to subdue the beast. Only then can we control its power."

As the leaders strategized, murmurs of "terra" and "glacier" floated through the lower court, mingling with the enigmatic mention of "Niflheimir." The courtiers in the lower court exchanged bewildered glances, their intrigue sparking rumors while the wise knew enough to conclude the truth of their devilish plans and also knew enough to not oppose it.

As Vulcan and Ragnor descended from the elevated court, their posture exuded authority and a sense of solemn responsibility. Their heads were held high, their expressions determined, and they avoided meeting the gazes of those in the lower court. Whispers and murmurs trailed after them as they exited the grand hall.

In the courtyard outside, Vulcan turned towards the path leading to his son's palace, his steps purposeful and deliberate. His mind was consumed with the weight of the decisions made in the court, the gravity of their plan settling heavily on his shoulders. Ignatius awaited him, and Vulcan knew he must impart the next steps to his son with caution.

Meanwhile, Ragnor moved with purpose toward his palace, his thoughts racing as he considered the implications of their alliance with the Inferno Dominion. He needed to convene with Fulminari Volta, his daughter and leader of the Thunderlash tribe, to prepare for the mission ahead. The notion of kidnapping the leaders of the other clans weighed heavily on his conscience, yet the necessity of their actions left him with little choice.

The Bestowed Comrade

As Cassian ventured further, the trail of smoke ahead stirred a mix of curiosity and apprehension within him. He kept a watchful eye on the surroundings, his confidence buoyed by the presence of the warrior at his side. They traversed under colossal peaks that seemed to kiss the sky, yet to Cassian's surprise, the air was not as bitterly cold as he had anticipated for the Cryoros Mountains.

The mountains, instead of being pristine white, were rugged and brown, with only scant remnants of thin ice clinging to their slopes. The caves they passed through lacked the characteristic icicles and frost that Cassian associated with the Glacierborns' homeland. It all seemed peculiar for a place he had imagined to be frozen and majestic.

Amidst this unusual landscape, the scene of devastation grew more apparent. Cassian noticed the remains of looted and burned homes, and the ground was littered with the charred bodies of fallen warriors.

Cassian turned to the warrior, his expression a mix of concern and inquiry. "What happened here?" The warrior's somber gaze met his, a silent acknowledgment of the tragedy that had befallen her people.

The warrior's demeanor shifted abruptly, her eyes welling with tears as she halted in her tracks. "It was her," she replied, her voice trembling with emotion. "Fulminari Volta led a massive army that swept through these lands, leaving destruction in its wake."

Cassian's expression darkened with concern. "But how could the Glacierborns, so powerful in their own right, fall to such devastation?"

The warrior shook her head, struggling to compose herself. "Fulminari is a force of nature herself. She breached our defenses effortlessly, her troops overpowering us at every turn."

Cassian's mind raced with questions. "What was her goal? Why attack with such force?"

The warrior's voice caught in her throat; her eyes filled with grief. "She reached the heart of our civilization," she continued, her words choked with sorrow. "There, she committed the unimaginable..."

The weight of her unspoken words hung heavy in the air as the warrior's tears flowed freely, her silence speaking volumes of the tragedy that had befallen her people. Cassian stood in solemn silence, grappling with the gravity of the situation.

"We must press on," the warrior finally managed, her voice steadier. "To the heart of the Cryoros Mountains."

Cassian and the warrior continued their arduous trek through the scarred landscape of the Cryoros Mountains.

As they approached the remnants of what once was a bustling market area, the acrid scent of smoke lingered in the air, a haunting reminder of the recent devastation.

Cassian, his eyes scanning the ruins, spoke softly, "What happened here? Why would Fulminari Volta unleash such destruction?"

The warrior's expression darkened, a mixture of grief and anger evident in her eyes. "It was a ruthless act," she replied, her voice heavy with emotion. "Fulminari led her forces through our city, pillaging and burning everything in their path. This was once the heart of our civilization."

Cassian, troubled by the senseless destruction, pressed further, "But why? What purpose does it serve?"

The warrior paused; her gaze fixed on a charred structure that had once been a bustling merchant's stall. "We don't know for certain," she admitted, her voice tinged with frustration. "It may be a tactic to weaken us, to instill fear and dependence."

As they navigated through the ruins, the warrior pointed to a shattered stone archway that marked the entrance to what was likely a grand plaza. "This was where our people gathered," she explained, her voice tinged with nostalgia. "Now it lies in ruin."

Cassian surveyed the devastation, his mind racing with questions.

"Another clan, the Terrashifters, suffered a similar fate" the warrior continued. " Ignatius led a cavalry to their lands," she recounted, her voice filled with sorrow. "They faced destruction just as we did."

Cassian clenched his fists, his resolve hardening. "We cannot allow this to continue," he declared, his voice firm. "Their suffering is unprovoked, and they deserve justice."

The warrior placed a comforting hand on Cassian's shoulder. "We must prepare for whatever challenges lie ahead. For now, we must refill our energy for another day of arduous trekking."

As Cassian and the warrior set up camp, the sun began its descent, casting a warm golden glow over the rugged landscape. Cassian, curious about the devastation they had witnessed, turned to the warrior with a thoughtful expression.

After they relaxed, the warrior began "After the brutal assault on our people, many lives were lost, and our cities lay in ruins. Yet, we were spared total annihilation because the Inferno Dominion and Thunderlash see value in our powers. The Glacierborns' ability to control ice is indispensable during the scorching summers, providing relief and entertainment. Likewise, the Terrashifters' skills in shaping earth are exploited for mining jewels and constructing structures."

Cassian listened intently; his gaze fixed on the flickering flames of their campfire.

Cassian: "So, they do not wish to fully eradicate your kind?"

The warrior nodded solemnly and said "They wish to weaken us to a point that we are incapable of rebelling". The warrior said after a solemn pause "That is my theory. Right now, with our leaders gone, our clans had to unite and pool our resources at the connecting edge of our territories and build a stronghold. Together, we stand stronger, having combined the power of the FrostHammer and the TerraSpear to form a stronghold that is potentially impenetrable, but the disappearance of our strongest members has left us vulnerable. We continue to collect warriors and regain strength pretty well and our core powers are well restored at the central stronghold."

Cassian sat beside the crackling campfire, the dying light of the sun giving way to the sparkling stars above. As the peaceful night settled in, his mind involuntarily returned to the searing pain of his rune, accompanied by the memory of a vanishing star. He shook off the unsettling recollection and turned his attention to his companion and asked, "What's your name?"

The warrior, tending to the campsite, paused, and looked up at Cassian with a faint smile and replied "My name is Eira. I am the heir to the throne of the Glacierborns, daughter of our kidnapped leader and heir to the throne."

Cassian's eyes widened in surprise at Eira's revelation. He said feeling let down "Why didn't you tell me earlier? Why would you hide that, Your Majesty……?

"It's hard times that hardened me, it is hard to be open now, with regular threats of total annihilation of my clan." Eira said with a dismissive smirk.

"What's your name, where do you hail from?" Eira asked inquisitively.

Cassian came forth hesitantly "I am Cassian, Cassian Vulcan, son of Ignatius and Fulminari. You could say I was the monumental failure of the revered and feared Thundering Flame Alliance."

Eira shot up from her makeshift bed and got into her fighting stance. She shuffled back rapidly and shouted "YOU TRAITOR! I should have known not to trust you." Eira wasted no more time. She ran and lunged toward Caspian, an icicle spear forming in her hand ready to attack, just when Cassian jumped to the side.

The skilled warrior was too fast for Cassian, but Cassian shouted back in the nick of time, "WAIT! I am not who you think I am. I might be the son of your arch nemesis, but I am unlike those evil selfish minded warmongers. I am nothing like them."

Cassian pointed to his shoulder and neck as he said again "See! I do not have a rune, and I do not have their powers either. I am but a failed strategy for my clans. They are the ones that exiled me, their own son, for being useless in war, without remorse. I hate them as much as you do, Eira, understand me."

Eira, still shocked and paranoid, "I get why you would not tell that to me earlier, and I apologize for assuming and calling you a traitor, a spy. It is just that these recent events have brought upon me a lot of responsibility and as a result, I have become colder, more defensive."

Cassian sighed from relief.

"Cassian, then what power do you actually possess?" Eira asked.

"I am confused. I don't have a power rune, thus no power but I have this strange empty Eye like rune on my back" he turned slowly as he pointed to the centre of his back.

Eira's reaction to Cassian's revelation was nothing short of profound astonishment. She stumbled backward, her eyes wide with disbelief, and then dropped to her knees, as if the weight of Cassian's truth was too immense to bear standing. For a moment, the world seemed to hold its breath along with her, the silence broken only by the crackle of fire and the soft sigh of wind around their tents.

Slowly, Eira bowed her head in reverence, her voice barely more than a whisper as she spoke words that carried the weight of centuries of tradition and faith. "In these grave times," she began, her tone tinged with solemnity, "I looked towards the gods for guidance and aid."

As a princess of the Glacierborns, Eira had been granted access to the sacred library of their palace, where her education included the ancient tales of the creators and watchers—the Starweavers. These celestial beings were said to oversee Sköllgard and countless other realms, bearing a distinctive rune, an eye-like symbol on their backs that signified their divine purpose.

Cassian's mind raced, trying to comprehend the implications of Eira's words. His heart pounded in his chest, a mixture of anxiety and wonder washing over him. Eira's next revelation was like a bolt of lightning in the night, illuminating the darkness of his uncertainty. "But your eye rune is empty," she continued, her voice trembling with awe, "which means you must be... deemed."

The weight of those words hung heavy in the air, leaving Cassian speechless. He waited, his breath caught in his chest, as Eira's gaze turned skyward. With a voice filled with both desperation and hope, she called out into the dark expanse above, "Astraeus!"

For a moment, nothing happened. The silence stretched, thick and palpable. Then, as if in response to Eira's invocation, the earth itself seemed to tremble. A swirling vortex tore open the ground between them, an otherworldly portal that defied all sense of natural order. Out of this tumultuous void stepped a figure, cloaked in shadows and radiating an aura of ancient power.

The newcomer emerged from the portal with an air of enigmatic authority. His eyes, deep and inscrutable, surveyed Cassian with a knowing gaze. "Eira," he spoke, his voice a low rumble that resonated with a mysterious energy, "you called, and I have come."

To Forge
A Warrior

In a secluded, marshy expanse of Cassian's homeland, Ragnor and Vulcan convened under the dense canopy of ancient trees. This untouched area, shielded by a thick canopy, seemed to guard an ancient relic—one that the wise and elders prayed would never be wielded again. It was this relic that had once caused the rifts between Sköllgard and the realm of the nature gods.   Ragnor's daughter, Fulminari, and Vulcan's son, Ignatius, had just returned from a successful expedition to procure the clan leaders of the Terrashifters and Glacierborns. They together with the leaders had also been fairly successful with subduing the giant creature and dragging it to the most secure holding cell of Sköllgard, The Dungeon of the Thunderlash tribe—a subterranean labyrinth, built aeons ago beneath the weight of a colossal plateau. The dungeon itself was a daunting structure, deep and cavernous, lined with relics and the remains of warriors' long past.

The unconscious creature was held in the dungeons. The creature was a towering monstrosity, its body covered in thick, jagged plates of obsidian-like armor that seemed to absorb all light.

The monstrous creature and its powers were of no use if they could not be directed by a fearless warrior. Using their formidable powers, Vulcan and Ragnor unsealed a magically concealed cave entrance—a massive boulder that required their combined strength to move aside. Beyond the threshold, the cave revealed itself to be a mystical and unseen passage, imbued with a strange, intoxicating energy that only the strong-willed could resist.

As they ventured deeper, a soft, mystical white fog enveloped them, illuminated by the glow of a lamp-like artifact. The relic shone with an otherworldly brilliance, and both Ragnor and Vulcan approached it with utmost reverence. They carefully retrieved the artifact and carried it back to the Thunderlash dungeons, their minds focused on their goal.

Their victory hinged on absolute control over the dragon. To achieve this, they needed someone of unparalleled strength—someone who could rival the power of the Craftweavers themselves, someone who was war minded, wise, calm, powerful, and had prowess in all forms of elemental control and combat. Their solution lay in the ancient relic, which held the key to igniting the White-Flamed Eternal Fire.

However, this plan required a sacrifice of unimaginable magnitude. Ragnor and Vulcan sought to convince their respective children, Fulminari and Ignatius, to offer themselves to the divine fire along with the clan leaders they procured—a sacrifice that would bring forth a being born of the gods' blessing, a being who had the wisdom of Fulminari, Battle sense of Ignatius, strength of the terrashifters, and self-control of the Glacierborns, along with the powers of them all. THE PERFECT SPECIMEN.

In preparation for this sacred ritual, Ragnor and Vulcan entered a three-month period of penance and meditation. Their prayers were answered by a nature god, granting them the divine will to proceed. With unwavering determination, they readied themselves for the profound and perilous ritual that would reshape the fate of Sköllgard.

Reclaiming
The Throne

Astraeus introduced himself to Cassian, he spoke with an air of mystery and wisdom. "I am Astraeus," he began, "known to few and yet knowing all. I am a child of the Nulls, those without elemental powers, who proved myself by navigating the Forest of Wisdom alone, without aid or magic."

Astraeus stood taller than Cassian. He had a lean and lanky build, with an air of agility and precision in his movements. Draped over his left shoulder and arm was a leopard hide, its spotted fur a striking contrast to the rest of his attire. The remainder of his clothing was fashioned from wolfskin, giving him a wild and rugged appearance.

A sideways leather bag was strapped around him, resting against his hip. It looked well-worn, hinting at the many journeys it had accompanied him on. Dangling from his waist were small, shuriken-like weapons, glinting in the light. His presence exuded a mixture of mystique and danger.

Astraeus revealed his remarkable award to Cassian, the Galactic Hand, by pulling back a leopard-skin covering on his left hand. Cassian's eyes widened as he beheld a wondrous sight—Astraeus's hand appeared as if it were a patch of space itself, adorned with stars, galaxies, and cosmic wonders. "With this hand," Astraeus explained, "I can traverse the universe, traveling wherever I desire through portals of my creation. I can even take others with me."

Curious about why Eira had called upon him, Astraeus turned to Cassian and noticed the empty rune on his back. Chuckling softly, he remarked, "Ah, now we understand. He has returned, though the world remains unaware. Your deeming is not yet complete, Cassian. To achieve this, you must journey to the home realm of the Starweavers— the Nexus."

Eira nodded, her expression serious yet determined. "Cassian's rune burns when a star vanishes. We believe there is a connection, a destiny intertwined with the fabric of the cosmos."

Astraeus fixed his gaze on Cassian. "Indeed, Cassian. The Nexus holds the key to your purpose, your power, and the mysteries of the stars. Are you prepared for the journey ahead?

We must go swiftly, The Thundering Flame Alliance is mustering for war, and we need someone of great strength to protect us, I am but a traveller."

Cassian felt a surge of determination. "I'll go," he declared. "If my destiny lies in the Nexus, then I must face it head-on."

With a deep breath, Cassian turned to Astraeus. "Lead the way."

Astraeus raised his cosmic hand, and before them, a swirling portal materialized. It shimmered with interstellar colors, beckoning them into the unknown.

Eira placed a reassuring hand on Cassian's shoulder. "Remember, Cassian, you carry the hopes of the Glacierborns. Find your answers in the Nexus and return to us stronger than ever."

With resolve burning in his heart, Cassian stepped forward with Astraeus, he entered the portal—a gateway to the realm of the Starweavers and the mysteries of the cosmos.

As they traversed through the cosmic portal guided by Astraeus, he began to explain the dire situation unfolding in Sköllgard.

"Ahead lies the Nexus, but we must be prepared," Astraeus cautioned. "The Thundering Flame Alliance is amassing its forces for war. They have harnessed the power of the Giant Serpent from Niflheimr Lake, a creature of immense strength and fury. But their most formidable weapon is the warrior produced by the Eternal Divine White Flame who has the prowess of all elements and the experience and skill of the strongest members of all tribes—a warrior potentially stronger than the Giant Serpent itself."

Cassian's eyes widened at the gravity of the situation. "How can we stand against such power?"

Astraeus's expression was grim yet determined. "We must uncover the secrets of the Nexus. Within its halls, we may find the knowledge and strength needed to thwart their plans."

Eira, ever resolute, nodded in agreement. "The Starweavers possess ancient wisdom. If anyone can guide us, it is they."

Cassian and Astraeus emerged from the mystical vortex onto unfamiliar terrain—a colossal hall adorned in white and gold. The grandeur of the hall was evident, but it bore the marks of time and distress. The once-lustrous white walls seemed pale, with cracks running through them like the veins of an ancient, weary giant. The golden embellishments had lost their sheen, rust creeping over them, a testament to the trials faced by its inhabitants.

The hall was filled with ethereal beings, their forms ghostly and translucent. They sat on either side of the grand aisle, their heads sunk in despair. Their expressions were weary, eyes hollow from endless waiting and suffering. Yet, as Cassian entered, a collective shift occurred. Slowly, they raised their heads, eyes filled with a glimmer of hope. It was as if they had been waiting for this moment, for him, to break the cycle of despair.

Cassian's eyes were drawn to the center of the hall, where a grand throne stood, conspicuously empty. The throne itself, though majestic, showed signs of neglect, its intricate carvings dulled by layers of dust and age. Yet, it emanated a powerful aura, as if it had been waiting for someone to reclaim it.

A voice, distinct from that of Astraeus, resonated from behind him. "Walk forward, Cassian. Take your rightful place upon the throne."

Cassian turned to see a figure that looked remarkably like himself but with a radiant, ethereal glow. "Who are you?" he asked, a mix of curiosity and awe in his voice.

The figure stepped forward. "I am Eldris, your guardian." he declared, his voice carrying an otherworldly authority.

Cassian was taken aback. "My guardian? What does this mean?" he asked, his mind racing with questions.

Eldris regarded him with a knowing gaze. "You possess a destiny intertwined with the cosmos, Cassian. Embrace your role, for the fate of Sköllgard hinges upon your actions."

Cassian hesitated but felt a pull toward the throne. He walked forward, each step resonating with a sense of purpose. As he approached, the beings on either side bowed their heads in reverence, acknowledging his presence.

"Why does this throne look so familiar?" Cassian murmured to himself.

Eldris answered, "It is because your soul has always belonged here. The Nexus has awaited your return for years."

Cassian reached the throne and paused, looking back at Eldris. "What must I do?"

"Sit upon the throne and claim your birthright. Only then will your true journey begin" Eldris replied.

Cassian took a deep breath, steeling himself. He turned and slowly lowered himself onto the throne. As he did, a surge of energy coursed through him, connecting him to the very fabric of the universe.

The rune on his back, instead of burning, started to shine with a brilliant, otherworldly light. He felt a surge of energy coursing through him, revitalizing every fiber of his being. The sensation was overwhelming, and he slipped into unconsciousness, his mind drifting into a deep, serene void.

It felt like only a moment later when Cassian awoke, but everything had changed. He looked down at himself, astonished. He was no longer the frail boy he had been he was now tall, muscular, and lean. His sickness had vanished, replaced by a newfound strength and vitality. In his excitement, he jumped down from the throne, landing with such force that the ground cracked beneath him. As he stepped forward, the ground repaired itself, mirroring the restoration of his own body.

Cassian's heart raced with exhilaration. He flexed his arms, feeling the immense power within. He turned to Eldris; eyes wide with wonder. "What is this? What has happened to me?" he asked, his voice filled with awe.

Eldris watched him with a serene smile. "This is not the pinnacle of your power, Cassian. It is only the very beginning. You have attained the physical power of a true Starweaver."

Cassian felt a sense of destiny settling upon him. "A true Starweaver? What does that mean?"

Eldris stepped closer, his gaze unwavering. "You are the chosen one, Cassian. Reborn as the leader of the Starweavers. You are next to the throne after Aegir the Supreme. Your journey has just begun."

Cassian absorbed this information, his mind racing. "What must I do to complete my journey?" he asked, determination etched into his features.

"You must meet the trio," Eldris explained. "The Starweavers, the Craftweavers, and the Loreweavers. Only then will you fully awaken your powers and fulfill your destiny."

Eldris turned to Astraeus, his expression solemn. "I trust you to guide Cassian on his path. Ensure he meets the trio and learns from each of them."

Astraeus nodded, his galactic hand shimmering with starlight. "I will guide him," he promised. "We will ensure that Cassian fulfills his destiny."

Eldris nodded. "I trust you to lead him well."

Nemesis Awakened

The ritual was complete, and after the sacrifice, a 12-year-old child was born to them. They named him Cillian Vulcan. He possessed the powers of all the clan members and bore all their runes. His build was exactly like Cassian's, but his face was more rugged and ruthless. He was given the sword of the Inferno Dominion, a weapon of immense power.

In a grand ceremony, the elders of the Thunderlash tribe brought forth the giant serpent, Thraex. The serpent had been infused with the power of the Thunderlash Trident, a legendary weapon. The trident's powering blue jewel was embedded in the serpent's neck, imbuing it with the ability to spew thunder projectiles.

The wise and elderly of both clans gathered around Cillian and the serpent. They drew an intricate rune on both Cillian and Thraex, using ancient, sacred ink. The rune glowed with a mystical light, connecting their minds in a profound bond. This connection allowed Cillian to command the serpent as effortlessly as if it were another limb, making them a formidable duo.

Cillian stood tall, his Obsidian eyes reflecting a fierce determination. The serpent rose with Cillian at its crown, its scales shimmering with a blue hue from the embedded jewel. The clans watched in awe as the boy and the serpent moved in perfect synchronization, a testament to the immense power now wielded by their new leader. With Cillian Vulcan and Thraex, the Thunderlash and Inferno Dominion had created a force capable of shifting the balance of power in Sköllgard forever.

Cillian and the serpent, Thraex, began their conquest with a calculated and ruthless strategy. Their first target was a neighboring civilization of the Nulls, a people with no elemental powers but under the sworn protection of the Glacierborns. With the Glacierborns decimated, the few remaining warriors were no match for Cillian and Thraex.

At dawn, Cillian and Thraex approached the Null settlement. The serpent moved silently through the early morning mist; its presence hidden by the dense forest. As the first light of day began to break, Cillian signaled for the attack.

Thraex struck first. The serpent's immense strength demolished the outer defenses with ease. Its powerful, glowing blue jewel unleashed a torrent of destructive energy, tearing through the walls and scattering the defenders. Cillian, riding atop Thraex, guided its movements with precision, ensuring key targets were swiftly neutralized.

With the defenses in ruins, Cillian and Thraex entered the settlement. The Nulls, already demoralized by Thraex's assault, quickly fell back. Cillian's leadership was evident as he directed Thraex with cold efficiency, focusing on capturing strategic points and securing the settlement's resources.

Once the settlement was under control, Cillian implemented strict measures to ensure loyalty. He established a network of spies and informants among the Nulls to root out dissent and gather intelligence on the status of the Glacierborns and Terrashifters. He sent his spies at a distance of about two days' journey to the last known stronghold of the Glacierborns, ensuring they could monitor any movement or regrouping.

The legend of Cillian Vulcan and the serpent Thraex spread quickly, instilling fear in other settlements. The combination of Cillian's strategic mind and Thraex's unmatched power made them an unstoppable force. The Nulls of the east, now under his rule, served as both subjects and spies, ensuring Cillian remained informed about any potential threats.

Cillian's dominion expanded as he solidified his control over the Nulls of the east. Cillian now wished to traverse to the southern settlement of nulls to gather an army and get closer to the burning deserts of the terrashifters.

Fit For a King

"We must hurry," Astraeus said as they traversed through the portal, urgency lacing his voice. "The Thundering Flame Alliance is preparing for war, and they have weapons and powers that are beyond anything we've faced before."

Cassian, still trying to process everything, looked at Astraeus with a mix of curiosity and concern. "What do you mean? What kind of powers are we talking about?"

Astraeus took a deep breath. "They have the dragon, Thraex. This beast is no ordinary creature. Thraex was infused with the power of the Thunderlash trident. The blue jewel embedded in its neck allows it to channel devastating energy blasts, capable of tearing through the strongest defenses. It moves with a speed and strength that can flatten entire armies in minutes."

Cassian's eyes widened. "A dragon infused with elemental power. That sounds unstoppable."

"It nearly is," Astraeus continued. "But that's not all. They have Cillian Vulcan, born from the eternal white flame, possessing the powers of all the clan members and their runes. Cillian is unlike any warrior we've ever seen. He's agile, incredibly strong, and can control Thraex with his mind, thanks to the rune that connects them. This makes him capable of coordinated attacks that are both strategic and devastating."

Eira, listening intently, added, "Their initial conquest was a test of their power. They attacked the Nulls, a civilization with no elemental powers but protected by the Glacierborns. The Nulls stood no chance. Cillian and Thraex took over swiftly, leaving no survivors among the warriors and spreading fear among the survivors."

Astraeus nodded. "Cillian has set up spies to monitor the Glacierborns and Terrashifters. He is cunning and strategic, ensuring they remain weakened and incapable of mounting a resistance. He uses the resources of the Nulls to fortify his position, preparing for further expansion."

Astraeus and Cassian approached the domain of the Craftweavers and suddenly emerged from the ground. They found themselves in a well-lit, small cave that forced Astraeus to bend down due to its low ceiling. The cave was filled with blue-skinned dwarven beings, all of whom were busy with their tasks. Directly ahead, they saw many workers surrounding a huge pit of lava, dipping something into the molten pool. To their left, a small hall led up to a ginormous workshop filled with gigantic gears, claws, and boulders working continuously. The air was filled with the continuous creaking, falling, banging, and thudding noises.

Cassian looked around in awe, trying to take in the sheer scale and complexity of the place, but Astraeus stood calm and still. Cassian, feeling restless, finally shouted out, "Excuse me!" The entire workshop came to an ominous stop; all sounds ceased, leaving a total silence. Cassian felt embarrassed, realizing he might have done something wrong.

Just then, a dwarf, slightly smaller than the others but more decked with armour, walked out. He approached Cassian and simply asked, "Let me see your back, child." Cassian hesitated but turned around. Suddenly, he felt a searing pain in his scar. He spun around, ready to attack, but the dwarf was gone.

Astraeus grabbed Cassian and told him his back was touched with a burning piece of metal and he need not be scared. Then they fell through another portal. Cassian was surprised, scared, and confused. "What just happened?" he asked, his voice trembling.

Astraeus replied calmly, "You will know in due time, Cassian. It had to be done quickly so that you wouldn't protest against it. Trust me, it was necessary."

Cassian's mind raced with questions, but he trusted Astraeus. As they dived through another portal, he couldn't help but think about what the encounter with the Craftweavers truly meant for his destiny.

Cassian and Astraeus stepped through another portal, expecting to return to Sköllgard. When they emerged, they found themselves in a dense forest. Cassian looked around in confusion before asking, "Where are we?"

Astraeus replied, "This is the land of the Loreweavers. It was here that I proved my worth by navigating the entire forest without powers or help. For my bravery, I received the blessing of the Galactic Hand."

Astraeus guided Cassian forward. At first, Cassian saw nothing but rubble, but he followed without question. As they approached, the rubble rearranged itself into a gate. They stepped through and found themselves in a very cold landscape. Cassian was astonished and in awe at the sight. They were at the peak of a mountain.

Ahead, they spotted a man in simple white clothing, sitting calmly. The man looked at Astraeus and smiled, then beckoned Cassian forward with a silent gesture. Cassian approached, and the man produced a scroll from behind him. In a deep, ancient, clear voice that resonated like a giant's, he shouted, "KRONOS!"

The scroll blasted apart, and a feather dipped in red ink fell into the man's hand. He used it to write something on Cassian's forehead. Cassian Cassian suddenly went unconscious and to Cassian it felt like years but in reality, he was back in a matter of seconds.

The man said before he bowed, "Blood memory". Cassian and Astraeus fell through another portal, falling towards Sköllgard.

They landed near Eira and saw her pointing to something in tears. Bothe Cassian and Astraeus looked up only to see a dark figure in the distance standing over something. Astraeus gasped under his breath " Thraex… and Cillian".

Cillian's Illusion

Cillian and Thraex, after conquering the Nulls of the East, now set their sights on a strategic position: the Southern Nulls, who were protected by the Terrashifters. They launched a ferocious attack at dawn, with Thraex's fiery breath scorching the earth and Cillian wielding his elemental powers to unleash devastating lightning strikes. The Terrashifters, though resilient, were quickly overwhelmed by the relentless onslaught. Thraex's claws tore through their defences, and Cillian's precise attacks left no room for retaliation. Within hours, the Southern Nulls fell, their protectors defeated.

With this victory, Cillian now commanded a massive army ruled by fear. He began preparations for an all-out assault, with more soldiers marching in from the Northern Null civilization. The army swelled in numbers, and the Nulls, driven by terror and subjugation, prepared for the upcoming battle. Cillian and Thraex, confident in their power, focused on honing their strength.

"We'll crush them easily," Cillian thought, his eyes glinting with ruthless ambition. "With my elemental powers and Thraex's might, we'll annihilate the

Terrashifters and Glacierborns. The Nulls will enslave the survivors, and our dominance will be unchallenged."

As the preparations continued, the atmosphere was thick with anticipation and dread. The once-peaceful regions now trembled under the looming shadow of Cillian's army. The final confrontation was imminent, and Cillian's overconfidence only fueled his determination to achieve total conquest.

But he had no idea what was about to come his way.

Memories Of Aegir

Cassian was astonished at the sheer size of the serpent, Thraex. It was much larger than he had imagined, its scales glistening ominously under the pale light. The aura of the man standing atop it, Cillian, was intimidating, befitting someone who shared Cassian's blood.

"How did he gain the powers of all four clans?" Cassian asked, his voice steady but filled with curiosity.

Astraeus, standing beside him, explained, "There was a ritual involving the Eternal Divine White Flame and a great sacrifice. Cillian was born from that flame, a fusion of the strongest elements from each clan. Your blood is the same as his. You are half-brothers."

Cassian's eyes narrowed. "It doesn't matter. We may be brothers by blood, but we are opposites in will and action. I won't hesitate to stop him."

Astraeus nodded. "Your determination is admirable. But remember, he is powerful. You must be prepared."

Cassian's resolve hardened. "I'm not afraid of Cillian. He may have power, but I have something more valuable: experience."

Astraeus looked puzzled. "Experience? You haven't fought in a single battle."

Cassian's expression turned solemn. "In the brief moment of unconsciousness on the Loreweaver mountain, for me, three years passed. I relived the memories of Aegir the Supreme, mastering my abilities through rigorous training, understanding my rune and the significance of my scar. I gained a wealth of battle prowess and experience."

Astraeus's eyes widened in realization. "So, you have the wisdom and experience of Aegir himself?"

Cassian nodded. "I know every aspect of my power now. I understand what my rune means, why my scar burns, and I have the battle experience of a lifetime. I am ready to face Cillian."

There was a sudden loud bang in the distance. Cassian and Astraeus turned to see the protective dome built by the combined powers of the Terrashifters and Glacierborns. This formidable barrier, made of tightly fused ice and sand, was their last defence, sheltering the remaining survivors of both clans.

Even with its strength, the dome was weak against Cillian's relentless assault. He struck it with his molten fist, each punch accompanied by a crackling surge of lightning. The serpent, Thraex, joined the attack, its massive tail whipping against the dome with thunderous force. The bangs grew louder and more frequent as the onslaught intensified.

The scene was chaotic. The ground shook with each impact from Cillian and Thraex. Sparks flew and chunks of ice and sand crumbled from the dome with every strike. Cassian could feel the fear and desperation of the survivors who were helpless, but no longer.

Cassian could see the dome beginning to crack, the once impenetrable barrier showing signs of weakness. He felt a surge of urgency. "Brother," he said, turning to Astraeus, "can you open a portal in the sky?"

Astraeus nodded, understanding the gravity of the situation and trusting Cassian's instinct. He placed a hand on Cassian's shoulder, and in an instant, he was enveloped in a shimmering vortex. The world around him blurred, and when he emerged, he was directly above Cillian and the serpent.

Cassian was masterful at his art. He had received the powers to control something more than an element, the essence of creation of realms and the creator of all elements, Ether. Cassian could control a translucent reddish fluid from which he could create anything he imagined; its limits were his imagination. He used his experience and tactics to manifest a dragon with huge claws and giant wings. As the dragon came into existence made of Ether, Thraex noticed it and Cillian got to know immediately through their magical telepathy. Cassian dived down before Cillian could react and did the unpredictable, lifted off with Thraex in the claws of the conjured dragon so big that Thraex seemed like a child. Cassian knew that with the telepathy and powers of Thraex it would be stronger on ground but in a place like the sky where it could not even move itself, its sheer size and power would be nothing but useless. Cassian had jumped off the dragon when it came low to grab Thraex and landed right next to Cillian.

Cassian landed right next to Cillian, who was looking up at the sky for Thraex. Cassian called out, his voice filled with authority, "Hey, brother, stop it now."

Cillian turned, sneering. "What will you do? You think you can stop me? My powers have no bounds."

Cassian's gaze was steady. "I don't think so. I'm sure of it."

"Let's see what you're made of then," Cillian snarled, pulling back his fist to punch. Just a second before impact on the dome, Cassian surprised him by instantly creating a shield of ether around the dome. Ether, the supreme element of creation, was highly resistant to other elements and attacks. Cassian then lunged forward, closing the distance between him and Cillian.

Cillian saw no weapon in Cassian's hands and thought he could easily block the attack. However, Cassian had another trick up his sleeve. The scar burned into his back by the Craftweavers granted him the ability to materialize the perfect weapon for any situation at the moment of impact. As Cassian swung his right hand with full force, an axe formed in his grip, ready to cleave through Cillian. But as Cassian swung and rolled, he felt no resistance; his weapon had hit nothing.

Cillian, a masterful warrior and incredibly fast, had anticipated Cassian's move. He had dodged swiftly, sneaking behind Cassian. With a full-force punch using his molten fist, Cillian struck Cassian from behind. Cassian was pushed forward, stumbling, but he instantly rolled to get back up. Suddenly, a flash of lightning blinded him, leaving him vulnerable. He stumbled again and fell. Cillian then used his sword handed to him from Vulcan to deliver a fatal blow to Cassian's thigh.

Mocking Cassian, Cillian taunted, "You're no more than a weakling."

This enraged Cassian. Fuelled with determination, he shot up and cast ether around Cillian, leaving a small opening through which he thrust his hand. A sword materialized in his grip, aiming straight at Cillian. But before he could fully reach, the ground beneath him shook violently. The earth tore up, flinging Cassian upwards. He saved himself with an ether shield but missed his target once more, realizing Cillian had manipulated the earth to evade and counterattack.

Cassian landed a few meters away near Astraeus, panting. "Cillian is too strong," he admitted.

Astraeus, calm and resolute, said, "You were chosen for a reason, Cassian. You have people to save." He pointed to

Cillian, who was back to punch the dome. "It's not impossible. I have a plan."

Cassian, gathering his resolve, nodded. "What's the plan?"

Astraeus explained his strategy quickly and clearly. Cassian listened intently, his resolve hardening. He was ready to attack again.

Cassian first controlled his ether dragon and before Thraex could attack the dragon sunk it's claws deeper into Thraex and when it neared a mountain with a sharp peak it rose higher and then with a final dive the dragon pushed Thraex through the mountain piercing its core and then dragged it forward fully demolishing the beast. The ether dragon then melted away as if nothing was ever there.

The death of Thraex was a big tug in the core of Cillian, Cillian felt as if a part of himself left. Cillian was disoriented and using this moment, Astraeus opened a portal and sent Cassian through it. Astraeus shouted out to Cassian "Attack!!" and just then Cassian pushed his hand down with full force as he dropped out above Cillian, His hands now had a spear pointing to the centre of Cillian's head. Cillian barely dodged the spear, but it hit his foot. Cillian was in grave pain and as he shouted with rage a streak of lightning rocketed across the sky towards Cassian who fell through another portal and fell out behind Cillian.

Cassian nodded, his mind racing with strategies. He knew Cillian was formidable, but he also sensed his opponent's waning energy. Cassian remembered from his lesson about his powers from his 3-year training. He remembered that Ether shaped reality, so he can shape it too. He used this tactic to produce multiple copies of himself all around, mirroring his actions so flawlessly that it was impossible to discern the real from the created.

With a resolute shout, all Cassians surged forward, their hands ready with precision. Cillian, still recovering from his last attack, attempted to summon a wall of ice and sand, but Cassian's assault was relentless. Each strike was fueled by determination and honed skill, aimed to wear down his opponent's endurance, enhanced with the prowess and unexpectedness of portals opened by Astraeus.

Astraeus moved swiftly, creating intricate portals to disorient Cillian. The battlefield became a canvas of shifting realities, adding to Cillian's struggle to regain control. Through the chaos, Cassian pressed on, his attacks calculated and unwavering.

Cillian, realizing he was at a disadvantage, unleashed a massive wave of elemental power. Flames erupted, lightning crackled, and earth trembled under his command.

Cassian's focus remained unwavering, his movements guided by instinct and the memory of Aegir's training. He knew this was his moment to end Cillian's reign of terror.

Cassian was now close enough to deliver a blow, and Cillian was exhausted after he unleashed his strength and did not know what to expect. Cassian swung his hand left to right as a hammer materialized and hit Cillian square in the chest. Cillian was very well prepared for war, decked with armour, and that blow was only a dent to Cillian. Cassian began to understand Cillian's tactics at this point.

Cassian knew he had little time before Cillian attacked again. This time Cassian ran up a small mound of sand and lunged down towards Cillian. Cillian was amused by this tactic because he had ample time to prepare for the attack. Cillian had already planned his defence and offense. The moment Cassian leaped Cillian summoned a wall of sand and ice in front of him, between him and Cassian. He then readied his fiery sword and pierced it through the wall hoping to catch Cassian on the other side, and…. BANG!! Cillian was flung metres, thrown by the Ether wolfsbane that attacked him from behind. Cassian had already planned to stop his fall with his ether shield and he slid down safe to see Cillian stumble ahead.

Cassian was happy but knew not to get ahead of himself because he was facing a formidable opponent.

Cassian drew on the Ether, forming a protective shield around himself as he advanced. Cillian barely noticed him approaching and prepared to counter, but as Cillian swung his sword Cassian was quicker this time. He feigned a direct attack, then swiftly sidestepped, catching the dazed Cillian off guard. The moment Cillian was distracted, Astraeus created a portal beneath Cillian's feet, destabilizing him momentarily. As Cillian stumbled, Cassian seized the opportunity. He swung his weapon with precision, materializing an axe this time which severed Cillian's abdomen and stripped him of his armour. The impact sent shockwaves through the ground, stunning Cillian.

Cassian didn't waste a second. He summoned all his strength and aimed another blow, this time a spear, directly at Cillian's core. The spear connected, driving Cillian back. Enraged and surprised, Cillian retaliated with a fierce blast of molten energy. Cassian countered with an ether shield, absorbing the impact. Cillian was not done yet. He opened an unexpected rift through the ground between Cassian's legs causing him to fall. Astraeus was busy holding Cillian back and could not save Cassian. Cillian breathed a sigh of relief and started to walk towards Astraeus to complete his task. Astraeus tried to trick and confuse Cillian, but it was child's play now. Cillian got close to Astraeus and at the perfect distance froze his feet to the ground. He then took his flaming blade and pointed it to Astraeus' heart and charged on. An inch away from Astraeus' heart he felt a backward tug and was lifted off his feet by an ether falcon and dropped between the crevice he created.

Cassian then came and freed Astraeus. "How did you survive that?" asked Astraeus to which Cassian replied, "The Ether falcon that dropped Cillian in lifted me out".

The ground began to shake again as Cillian rose through the cracks. Cillian was visibly injured and weaker, yet he continued to attack.

Both Cassian and Cillian charged with utmost determination towards each other, Cassian Holding an Ether shield in his left hand and Cillian with his sword in his right hand.

They both charged and the force with which their bodies met sent ripples across the land. Cassian pushed Cillian with his shield and swung his right hand where a dagger materialised. Cillian dodged to his left and hit Cassian on his side but was also pushed back himself. Cassian fell to the ground with the impact and Cillian seized the opportunity to grasp Cassian with the sand and ice as he sent down a barrage of thunderstrikes. Cassian materialzed an Ox that pushed Cillian out of the trap while Astraeus recovered and redirected most of the thunder blows towards Cillian. Both warriors were equally beaten up. Cassian decided to use brains over brawn. He glanced at Astraeus who understood the signal. Cillian charged again and so did Cassian, but mere seconds from impact, Cassian ran into a portal and Cillian tripped forward hitting nothing. Cassian tore through a portal behind Cillian and Cassian charged forward, his dagger morphing into a sword of pure ether. He drove it into Cillian, who struggled to maintain his footing.

In a final, desperate move, Cillian summoned all his elemental powers, creating a massive explosion of fire, lightning, and earth. Cassian did not expect that, and took a huge blow, weakening him as his skin blew apart and he fell back. Both warriors were now down to their knees. Cillian had only taken a few spear hits, nowhere as much damage as having the power of all elements unleashed on oneself. Cassian could not move, and Cillian was charging, mostly walking, slowly toward him with his sword dragging along. He began to hoist his sword onto his shoulder when he noticed Cassian looking to his left. Cassian did not need to save himself. Cassian saw it happen. Just as Cillian turned a small portal opened and a sharp icicle like spear blew through with an unfathomable speed and swiftly pierced through Cillian's right eye and came out through his head with a splash of blood. Cillian fell down instantly, and so did all hope of tyranny in the lands of Sköllgard. Cassian lay back sliding off his knees into the warm sand. The Null soldiers of Cillian's army saw their master get impaled with the icicle and happily gave up their arms and accepted defeat. He blinked and he was back in Nexus, on Aegir's throne, now his throne. He heard Eldris in front of him say, "That is one realm you saved, one of the twelve in the cosmos."

Cassian blinked again and he was back in Sköllgard. He goes on to subdue all leaders of the Thundering Flame Alliance and restore peace and balance in Sköllgard by helping all communities prosper. He pledged protection to the Nulls and abolished slavery.